Here is a list of things
people have said about Nina Soni.

"Nina Soni is many things: Indian American, a list-maker, a word-definer, and a big sister. She is funny, observant, and smart, and she can also sometimes be a bit forgetful. The number one thing that Nina is? Loveable! I adore Nina and know readers will, too."

—Debbi Michiko Florence, author of
the *Jasmine Toguchi* series

"A perfect fit for readers who enjoy realistic fiction about friendship and self-discovery."

—*School Library Journal*

"…a flawed but refreshing and very likable protagonist…"
—*Booklist*

"A sweet and entertaining series opener about family and friendship."

—*Kirkus Reviews*

She's a

Phe-no-me-non means a happening or an event.

To Kathy Landwehr, with appreciation for her insight and love for Nina's adventures.

—K. S.

Published by
PEACHTREE PUBLISHING COMPANY INC.
1700 Chattahoochee Avenue
Atlanta, Georgia 30318-2112
www.peachtree-online.com

Text © 2020 by Kashmira Sheth
Illustrations © 2020 by Jenn Kocsmiersky

Edited by Kathy Landwehr
Design and composition by Adela Pons

The illustrations were rendered digitally.

Printed in February 2020 in the United States of America by Lake Book Manufacturing in Melrose Park, Illinois.
10 9 8 7 6 5 4 3 2 1 (hardcover)
10 9 8 7 6 5 4 3 2 1 (paperback)

HC ISBN: 978-1-68263-054-9
PB ISBN: 978-1-68263-209-3

Cataloging-in-Publication Data is available from the Library of Congress.

NINA SONI
SISTER FIXER

Written by **Kashmira Sheth**
Illustrated by **Jenn Kocsmiersky**

PEACHTREE
ATLANTA

CHAPTER ONE

Mom stood by the door and waved goodbye to my sister and me. "Have a good day. *Bahut Seekhna.*"

Every single day Mom reminds us to learn a lot at school!

Kavita blew kisses to Mom and stepped on my shoes.

I grabbed her hand. "Stop walking backward."

"Nina, don't forget to bring Kavita home with you," Mom said to me.

I waved at her without looking back. I had only forgotten my younger sister at school once. Now every single day Mom also reminds me to bring her home!

On this frosty spring morning our breaths cart-wheeled before disappearing. I held Kavita's mittened hand in mine.

As we walked down our street, Kavita burst out singing. *"I have been working on the railroad."*

Kavita likes to sing—nursery rhymes, songs, jingles from TV commercials. And her favorite, songs she makes up. Sometimes whatever she sings on the way to school earworms in my head.

There are many reasons Kavita likes to sing.

In-my-head list of why Kavita likes to sing

* Singing is like her, flowing and unstoppable.
* Kavita means poetry in Hindi, so singing is all mixed-up with her name.
* Singing gives her a chance to interrupt anyone, anytime, anyplace.

So Kavita, poetry, was singing and skipping. She was making her lungs work as hard as her legs.

Unlike Kavita, I like to make lists because lists help me keep organized.

Or-ga-nized means you keep things all straight, not zigzaggy in your head.

Most of the time I write down lists in my notebook called Sakhi.

Sakhi means friend in Hindi.

I've named my notebook because...why not? People name their pets, their stuffed animals, and their imaginary friends, so it's okay to name my notebook. And when I write in Sakhi, it's like sharing a secret with a friend.

Kavita was still singing. *"Someone's in the kitchen with Dinah. Someone's in the kitchen I know-oh-oh-oh. Someone's in the kitchen with Dinah, stomping on the old man Joe."*

"It's not 'stomping on the old man Joe.' It's 'strumming on the old banjo,'" I said.

"These are not nice people." Kavita stomped her foot and her backpack slid down. "That's why they don't strum an old banjo. They like to stomp on the old man Joe."

I adjusted her backpack. "That would be silly. It makes no sense."

"I told you, they are mean." She shook her head. "Anyway, songs aren't supposed to make sense. Does 'four and twenty blackbirds baked in a pie...when the pie was opened the birds began to sing' make sense?"

"Well, no. But this song is different."

"Why is this different?"

"I don't know why. It just is."

"Let's ask someone else." She looked around. Jay came out of his house at that moment.

"Jay, Jay," Kavita called.

He didn't hear her. Or ignored her. I couldn't tell which. Jay not only lived on our street, he was in my fourth-grade class. And he was my best friend.

"Jay Davenport! You better answer or else I'll tell your mom!" Kavita was so loud that I bet her teacher, Mrs. Jabs, heard her from school. Three blocks away.

He looked over his shoulder. "What?"

"Isn't it 'stomping on the old man Joe'?"

"What?" Jay's eyes flashed. "What did you say about my grandpa?"

Oh no! Jay thought Kavita was talking about stomping his grandpa Joe. The one he goes fishing with every weekend when the weather is nice.

"Not *your* grandpa, silly. I'm talking about the man in the song. You know the one who's in the kitchen with Dinah?" Kavita asked.

"No, I don't even know any Dinah. But if someone was stomping on my grandpa, I'd beat him up."

Kavita wiggled her hand out of mine. She put her hands on her waist and said, "Someone is stomping on the old man Joe, but that Joe isn't your grandpa. And you can't beat up a man in a song."

"I can too."

Jay was a fourth grader arguing with a first grader. But I stayed silent because I didn't want to get between my sister and my best friend.

Kavita folded her arms. "You can't beat up this Joe. You know you can't."

Jay started walking fast.

Kavita watched him. "How can Jay believe that you can beat up a man in a song?"

I love Kavita but sometimes my sister exasperates me.

> *Ex-as-per-ate* means she acts as if she is eating my peace.

I pulled Kavita along. "We'd better hurry or else we'll be late for school."

"What has happened to Jay?" Kavita asked.

We were only a block away from school and I didn't want any more discussion. I motioned my arm in a big circle. "Let's call it the fourth-grade phenomenon."

> *Phe-no-me-non* means a happening or an event.

It sounds better than the other two words because it is a twisty long word. Since I'm in fourth grade, I love to use twisty long words.

"Phenomagic?" Kavita asked.

"Phenomenon, not phenomagic."

"It sounds like magic. And I hope the weird magic goes away before we go to Jay's cabin," Kavita said.

Oh yes, the cabin!

I had forgotten that next week was spring break. Jay's family had invited us to spend a couple of days at Jay's grandfather's cabin up north. Grandpa Joe's cabin. He would be there too.

Oh no! What if Kavita sings "stomping on the old man Joe" while we're at Grandpa Joe's?

Kavita shook my arm. "We have to make Jay's weird magic go away with *our* magic."

I sighed. "I don't have magic, Kavita."

"Yes, you do. Remember? It's abracadabra, *jadu manter, choo manter*! Magic!"

By this time we were at school. Kavita sang, *"Jay's a magical magician, which nobody can deny,"* and ran to the playground.

I hoped Jay—or any other fourth grader—wasn't around to hear Kavita.

As I went down the school hallway, I wondered why Kavita was so weird. There must be something I could do to fix that.

Soon.

Before we go to Jay's cabin.

I made a list in my head of what made Kavita weird.

Here is my in-my-head list

* Kavita's singing makes her weird.
* Her made-up songs make her weirder.
* Her loud voice makes her weirdest.

On top of that, her singing embarrasses me, exasperates me, distracts me.

As an older sister I had to do something.

In-my-head list of possible Kavita fixes

* Maybe I can tell Kavita that her singing is not good for her throat.

* Maybe I can tell her that her made-up songs are not funny.

* Maybe I can tell her that her loud voice hurts everyone's ears.

* Maybe I can tell her that it would be better if she did something else. Like drawing, coloring, or painting.

* Maybe I can tell her that her artwork can make our world colorful and peaceful.

If I am successful, I can publish my results in a journal or a magazine. I could write a book about it. The title could be *Five Easy Steps to Fix a Sister* (*FESTFAS*). Then I could be the famous author of *FESTFAS*. As famous as any other author.

Anyway, today was Friday and we were going to Jay's cabin on Tuesday. I had three days to work on my project.

> One day has 24 hours. And 3 days x 24 hours = 72 hours.

Even taking time out for sleeping and eating, I would have enough time to work on Kavita. The best part was that after today we had no school. Even though I had known Kavita all her life, I should observe her more.

> To *ob-serve* means to really, really pay attention.

I also had to remember that Kavita was not only a singer but a stubborn singer. An everywhere singer. By everywhere singer, I mean, Kavita sings in the house, in our car, walking to school and back. She sings when she is showering or using a bathroom. And maybe even in her sleep?

I had a challenge.

Chal-lenge means something you must do because it is difficult but important.

And I love challenges.

CHAPTER TWO

To solve a problem, you really have to be a good observer.

Ob-ser-ver means someone who pays attention.

Right now I couldn't pay attention to Kavita, so I decided to pay attention to the kids in my class. I would even observe Ms. Lapin. It would be good practice.

In the hallway, Tyler and Jay were taking off their jackets. Jay wore a red T-shirt with large letters that said "Ask Me How to Dance." By the time I got closer, he was walking into the classroom. The dancing figure on the back of his T-shirt stared back at me.

"Hi, Nina," Tyler said.

"Hi o' hi," I replied, all singsongy. It was because in my head I was still singing *"stomping on the old man Joe."* I tried to push it away. It got replaced with *"Jay's a magical magician, which nobody can deny."*

Tyler gave me a look.

When I settled down at my desk, Jay leaned over and said, "See that stack of paper? I think we'll get our science quiz back."

"I was hoping we'd get it back after spring break," I said.

"Why? Are you worried?"

I couldn't answer him because the second bell rang. Ms. Lapin clapped her hands.

I stopped arranging my pencils and settled down.

"Class," she said. "I'll hand back your science

quiz in a few minutes. You all did well and I am very pleased with how much work you put in."

I glanced at Tyler. He smiled. It looked like a worried smile though. I smiled back. I wondered how my smile looked.

When Ms. Lapin handed our papers back, I covered my grade with my arm, elbow, and hand. I had a B.

A B+ to be exact, but it was not an A. I stashed it away.

For the rest of the class I sat up straight and looked at Ms. Lapin. I tried to pay attention as she talked about magnetism and the North Pole and the South Pole.

I kept nodding at her but somehow along the way I was only half listening. Even though my eyes were on Ms. Lapin, my mind was back to singing "*stomping on the old man Joe.*" It was driving me crazy. How could I stomp on the song and stop it from playing in my head?

I couldn't, and it made me mad 'o mad.

The class was over. Now I didn't need to stop my mind. Not until the next class started!

All morning I observed and wrote in my school notebook. Today my brain had no space for list making. Because the song, Kavita's silly song, was taking most of my brain space.

So here is the written list.

My Friday morning observations

* Kyle sharpened his pencil three times. The same one.
* Tyler didn't look so worried anymore. Did he get an A on the science quiz?
* Emma doodled five scary faces in her math notebook.
* Jay picked at a scab on his elbow until it came off. (I wanted to write "And he ate it," just to make this more interesting, but he didn't. I couldn't lie.)

* Ms. Lapin is really into math because she was so excited about fractions.
* Ms. Lapin used some great fraction examples like a pizza, a rectangular chocolate bar, and an orange.
* This made me excited about them too.
* Doing fractions, I figured out something important. I had three days to fix Kavita. That meant I could fix her 1/3 each day. (1/3 + 1/3 + 1/3 = 3/3 = 1)

✳✳✳

During lunch, my friend Megan sat by me. Megan is in Mr. Honshu's class, so, she and I eat lunch together because that is the only time we can sit and talk, share and eat. We swapped our lunches. She gave me two rice cakes and a cheese taco and I gave her my three spicy rotis with sweet, sour, and hot lime chutney.

Jay was sitting with Tyler, Kyle, and Kyle's older brother Nick and his friends. Jay stared at his school cafeteria food, looking disgusted. I bet it smelled disgusting, because the whole lunchroom smelled disgusting.

I leaned toward Megan and whispered, "You know how my sister sings all the time?"

"Yup."

"I'm going to fix that. Then I'm going to write a book called *Five Easy Steps to Fix a Sister*. *FESTFAS* for short."

She took a dainty bite of a roti. I could tell that she was thinking while chewing. "The title *FESTFAS* has a festive sound. I like it. But why do you want to fix Kavita's singing? It's so much fun!"

"It's not fun if you have to live with it."

"I know Kavita," she said. "It'll be challenging. Good luck."

"I guess. But I love challenges." I took a huge bite out of my rice cake.

Megan raised her left eyebrow. "Here comes another challenge."

I looked up just as Jay asked, "Hey, do you have any rotis?"

I turned to him but couldn't answer because I was still chewing. For a light, fluffy food, rice cakes sure fill up your mouth, especially when someone asks you a question.

"Too late. I already traded with Nina," Megan said.

"How come you never trade food with me?" he asked me.

"So I can have the mushy beans and gray peas from the school lunch? No thanks."

"It's better than the tasteless rice cakes you're eating."

"Jay, doesn't *your* mom make roti?" Megan asked.

Jay didn't answer.

Megan looked confused. "I thought she came from India. Didn't she?"

"Just because someone comes from India doesn't mean they have to know how to make roti. Okay?" Jay snapped. Then he walked away.

"Ouch," Megan said. "What did I say?"

I examined the last of the rice cake piece, wondering why I had traded with Megan. "His mom never makes roti. I don't think she knows how."

"I just assumed she did. Even you know how to."

"Hey, what's that supposed to mean?" I asked.

Megan shrugged. "You're only nine and if you know how to, shouldn't she?"

"Not really. You know how to make piecrusts but your mom doesn't."

"That's because I help my grandma make them. Ever since I was little."

"Exactly. I like cooking, and rolling roti is fun. Jay and I used to help my mom when we were little."

It gave me an idea. "You know, Jay already knows how to roll roti, which is the hardest part of making them. Maybe he could teach his mom."

Megan nudged me with her shoulder. "Jay is already irritated with me. So *you* should suggest that to him."

How could I advise Jay to teach his mom when I had just rejected his request for a roti? I looked at Megan's food. Which had been mine only a few minutes ago. "Are you going to be able to eat all three rotis?"

"If you want to give him one, that's fine."

"Jay," I called, waving my arm, even though he couldn't see me.

"What?" He looked over his shoulder.

I pointed. "Want a roti?"

"Sure."

I handed him the roti. His bitter-melon green eyes sparkled when he said, "Thanks!"

It made me happy.

As we walked back to our classrooms, I asked Megan, "Remember how I told you that we were going to Jay's grandpa's cabin next week?"

"Yeah. You're going to make roti there?"

"No. I was just wondering if I can fix my sister before that."

"Like in three days? It's a lot, but I think you can do it!"

Megan had a lot of confidence in me. Which was good. It's good to have friends who believe you can do stuff.

I was lucky. I had three friends who believed in me. Jay, Megan, and my notebook, Sakhi.

***

I was so glad we talked about fractions today, because when you break up your project into fractions, it doesn't seem daunting.

> *Daunt-ing* means so difficult that you don't want to do it.

When the final bell rang, I hurried out the door. Kavita was already sitting on a bench outside. Soon we were on our way home.

I had to fix my sister by Tuesday. If I started today, I could finish early.

Kavita stopped by the giant oak tree. "Nina, do you need to use the bathroom or are you going to throw up?"

"No and no." I pulled her hand. "Let's just keep walking."

"Then are we running away from a bear?"

I couldn't tell Kavita I only had a little more than three days to make her unweird. If I told her I was going to fix her, she would resist.

> *Re-sist* means not go along with my plan.

Since I didn't have an excuse ready, I took the first one that flashed through my mind: Jay's T-shirt that read "Ask Me How to Dance."

"I have to hurry up because I have to practice a dance."

"What kind of dance?" she asked.

"Um...a...beaver dance." I have a stuffed beaver called Lucky, so Kavita didn't find it that strange.

"Can you show it to me, please?"

"Sure. As soon as we get home."

"No, teach me now. Then we will rush home. And dance together."

"Like right now? Here?" I looked around. I didn't see anyone. Or even any pets. This was a no-neighbors, no-pets, safe afternoon.

So maybe it was okay to show Kavita one or two moves. It would make her happy and make my fixing project easier.

I dropped my backpack under an oak tree. I rubbed my hands, blew on them, and then shook them.

"Why did you do that? Is that part of the dance?" Kavita asked me.

I had no explanation for my actions. But I had a very good excuse. "I am pretending to be a beaver. Okay?"

"Oh," she said. "They shake their paws because they are usually wet and they don't want to dance with wet paws?"

"Exactly." Now I had to come up with a dance.

Thinking is a crazy thing. When you don't want to think, all the ideas run around your brain like squirrels gathering nuts. When you want to spot ideas and capture them, they hibernate in a brain cave.

Hi-ber-nate means go to sleep for a long time in a cave or underground.

"I'm ready," she said.

I put my hand to my head and caught an idea. "Now watch, Kavita. I'm only doing this once." I stuck out my belly, then I shimmied one way, then the other. Up and down the sidewalk.

Kavita's eyes grew wide with admiration. "Wow!"

She parked her backpack under the oak right next to mine. "Let me try once."

She stuck out her stomach and puffed up her cheeks.

"Why are you puffing out your cheeks?" I asked.

"Because I am a beaver who just ate a big branch and it's stuck in my mouth."

I rolled my eyes before I realized what I was doing. If Kavita saw it, she wouldn't like it. But like my beaver Lucky, I got lucky. Today, Kavita didn't notice. I guess when your cheeks are puffed up, you miss your sister's rolling eyes. "Steps," I said.

Kavita copied my moves perfectly, but she wasn't shimmying very well. "You're doing a wonderful job. Here, watch me shimmy once more," I said.

I stuck out my stomach extra far and wiggled, shimmying this way and that.

Someone giggled from the other side of the tree.

I stopped midshimmy. "How long have you been spying, Jay Davenport?"

CHAPTER THREE

Jay stepped forward. "I am Jaasoos Jay, the spy."

In second grade, Jay and I used to play a spy game. His name was Jaasoos Jay and mine was Jamadar Nina. We would hide behind a tree, bush, or fence and spy on our neighbors. Especially on Mrs. Crump. By spying we had figured out Mrs. Crump's daily schedules.

* Monday: laundry
* Tuesday: baking
* Wednesday: grocery

* Thursday: bingo and volunteering at a soup kitchen
* Friday: lunch with friends
* Saturday: gardening with Mr. Crump and dinner out with him
* Sunday: crossword puzzle and sudoku and a sitting nap on a chair

But that was long ago. Mr. Crump was now retired. So maybe Mr. and Mrs. Crump followed the same routine together? Should we spy to find out? I didn't say that out loud. "Jay, we are too old to play the spy game."

He laughed. "Says someone who dances on the sidewalk?"

I ignored him and turned to Kavita. "Are you coming or not?"

"You run home. I'll walk with magician Jay," she said.

Jay came closer. "Not only am I a spy and a magician, I'm a magical spy and a spying magician."

"A magical spy, a spying magician, that's what Jay is," Kavita sang.

Jay was carrying his jacket in one hand and he waved it at me. "Go on, Nina. Practice your dance. I'll bring Kavita home."

What happened? I wondered. This morning Kavita was upset at Jay and now she wanted to walk with him and was calling him "magical spy" and "spying magician." I guess that's what makes her weird. I had to fix that also. I didn't know how, though.

"But this morning my mom reminded me to bring her home."

"Your mom reminds you every day."

The problem with having a best friend is that you tell them everything about your life. Then they can use it to argue with you. Like now.

"Nina, tell Mom I'm learning a dance from Jay."

Kavita turned to Jay and pointed to him. "Show me the Lucky Beaver dance."

"Nina just showed it to you," Jay said.

"Your T-shirt says 'Ask Me How to Dance.' If you don't know how, or don't want to show it, then you can't wear the T-shirt. You have to give it to me."

"Why do you want his sweaty, gross shirt, Kavita?" I asked.

"That's why we have a washing machine."

"It won't even fit you."

"I can wear it as my sleep shirt, like you wear Daddy's," Kavita said.

"My mom gave me this shirt for my birthday and I'm not giving it away," Jay said.

Kavita was quiet. It was an unexpected relief. Like when you're starving and someone brings you a yummy snack. Maybe she was ready to go home after all.

"Anyway, I don't have to know some silly beaver dance to wear my shirt," Jay said.

"I didn't know this was a special shirt. You don't have to give it to me," Kavita said softly.

"Thanks, I guess," Jay mumbled.

"Jay, remember, it's not a silly beaver dance. It's the Lucky Beaver dance. I'll show you how to do it. I just learned," Kavita said.

"And now you're an expert?" Jay asked.

Kavita nodded. "Sure am!"

She grabbed Jay's arm. "First, let's do a stomping dance like the person in the kitchen with Dinah. But not on someone. Just on the sidewalk." With that, she stomped until her face turned sweaty.

Jay wiggled his arm out of Kavita's grip. "Not doing that."

But then Jay's face got a knowing look and his green eyes turned sparkly. "Wait! Kavita, now I get what you're saying about the song this morning." He laughed. *Tee-hee-hee, tee-hee-hee.*

"So it's 'stomping on the old man Joe,' right?" Kavita asked.

"Sure, why not? Whatever you say." He laughed again.

"What's so funny?" Kavita asked, but then she joined in with Jay's laughing.

Now the *tee-hee-hee, tee-hee-hee* of Jay and the *he-hee-hee, he-hee-hee* of Kavita were mixed together.

Great. I was with two kids under the oak tree laughing hysterically, as if a clown was tickling them.

"I'm going home," I said as I picked up my backpack.

"Bye." Kavita blew me a kiss.

"Let me show you my Lucky Beaver dance," Jay said to her.

I couldn't leave now. I had to watch Jay. After all, he saw me dance, and I had to get even.

He put his backpack under the tree and stepped back onto the sidewalk. Kavita folded her hands and watched.

Jay did some quick, hopping footwork, flailing his arms.

"No, no, no. That's not how Lucky dances. That's a scarecrow dance when a farm is on fire," I said.

"Scarecrow?"

"Yes. Lucky is a beaver. He's heavy, but graceful in water. And you dance like he's as skinny as a scarecrow."

"Nina's right." Kavita rounded her elbows, puffed up her cheeks, and stuck out her tummy. Then she wiggled and shimmied and ended her dance with five jumping jacks.

"Not bad," Jay said.

"If we don't go home, Mom will worry. Come on," I said, going after Kavita. She circled the tree as I chased her.

"Now can you do the Lucky dance the way I showed you, Jay?" Kavita asked.

Jay followed Kavita's steps.

I watched.

Then they both did it together.

I couldn't believe I was watching two crazy kids dancing on the sidewalk.

"You too, Nina," Kavita said. "Do Lucky."

"I already did."

"I bet she doesn't know how to do it the way you do Lucky," Jay said.

"I do too. I was the one who showed her." I slid off my backpack. I flung my jacket on top of it. Then I wiggled and shimmied and ended my dance with five jumping jacks. Even though I didn't think Lucky Beaver would be doing jumping jacks.

They watched in silence. When I was done, they clapped.

"Let's all Lucky together," Kavita said.

"No. If we don't get home now Mom's going to come looking for us."

"Oh." Jay must have realized he was also late because he ran ahead. Then he turned around, came back, grabbed his backpack, and sprinted away.

"That Jay is funny," Kavita observed.

"Yes," I agreed.

The rest of the way home, I wondered about our spending two days with Jay and his family. I knew Mom and Dad would have fun with the adults. Jay and I would have fun, too. But Kavita wouldn't have anyone to play with. That meant she would be with Jay and me. Oh no! To get attention, she might act even stranger than she usually does.

Then there was her singing. What if Kavita sang "stomping on the old man Joe" super loudly? And Grandpa Joe heard it?

Would he get upset?

It was his cabin we were visiting. And it was not a good idea to have our host be mad at us.

My fixing project was super-important.

CHAPTER FOUR

Mom was waiting on the front steps. "What took you so long?" she asked.

"We were Luckying," I said.

Mom looked puzzled. "What's that?"

"It's my Lucky Beaver dance. I was teaching Kavita how to do it. Then Jay came and—"

"Want to see it?" Kavita interrupted. "It's amazing." She handed Mom her backpack. "Come on, Nina."

So I also gave Mom my backpack. Then Kavita and I did the Lucky dance.

Mom handed us our backpacks. She clapped. "Lovely. But remember to always come home first and then go back out for Lucky dancing."

"When we get home, you always want us to eat a snack, and then you want us to tell you how our day went, and then you ask us to do our homework, and by that time it's evening. And evening isn't a good time for Lucky dancing," I said as we went into the house.

Kavita was not paying any attention to us because she was still dancing, with her backpack thumping her back.

"Why not?" Mom asked.

"Because Lucky likes to relax in the evening. Not dance."

Mom smiled. "I need to turn on the dryer. I'll be back in a minute," she said.

I picked up a Pink Lady apple from the basket on the kitchen counter, washed it, and bit into it. Yum.

"Lady Pink is okay, but I like Granny Smith apples better," Kavita said. "Nina, can you please give me a Granny Smith?"

"These are the only apples we have." I offered her one. "Take it or leave it."

"I don't want to take it, and I don't want to leave it," she said. Her big brown eyes filled with sadness.

I washed the apple, then covered it with a dish towel and mumbled, "Abracadabra, *jadu manter, choo manter,* change from a Lady to a Granny, from Pink to Smith." I handed her the apple.

Kavita's cheeks turned into two apples as her smile pushed them up. "How did you do that?" she asked.

"I magicked it," I said, folding the towel. "See how quickly the Lady turned into a Granny?"

She took a big bite and when she was done chewing, said, "It tastes like Granny, but it's still pink."

I nodded and took another bite of my apple.

The phone rang.

"*Elhho*," I answered.

"Hey, Nina. This is Megan." I guess she knows my mouth-full-of-food voice. "Why were you dancing on the sidewalk?"

I wanted to ask, "How did you know?" But my mouth-full-of-half-chewed-apple voice sounded like "*Ow dhid du tow?*"

There was silence at the other end. Maybe Megan is not so good at understanding my mouth-full-of-food voice after all. I finished chewing, gulped it down, and asked again. "How did you know?"

"I saw you from the bus. We all did. Kyle pointed you out and everyone in the bus looked except the kids who were sitting on the other side. They got up, but the driver yelled at them to sit down. I'm glad I was sitting on the right side. You know what I mean. It was the left side of the bus, but it was the right side to watch the dance. I was—"

"I wasn't dancing." I had to say it while Megan was still talking because her phone talk is very different from her regular one. On the phone, she could go on and on for an hour without a break.

"You sure were! I thought you were gathering material for your sister-fixer thingy and *FESTFAS* book. Like doing research, you know. You do like projects and research. Even when you don't have to do them for school. I didn't tell Kyle that, but I was certain that was why you were dancing. Did you find out if Kavita—"

"No, that wasn't the reason. Just forget about it, will you?" I took another juicy bite out of my apple.

"Forget what? Your project, or your dancing?"

Just when I wanted Megan to talk on, she waited for my answer. I shouldn't have taken such a big bite out of the apple. I chewed as fast as I could. I realized that chewing goes very fast when you aren't paying any attention to it, but really slowly when you are.

"Nina, are you there?"

Where would I be? Even though she couldn't see me, I rolled my eyes. "I just want you to forget about the Lucky dance."

"Lucky dance? You even have a name for it? So cool! Does it have to do anything with your Lucky Beaver? The part I liked the best was at the end. The part with jumping jacks. Kyle took a video and showed it to kids who—"

"He what?" I almost choked. "How did he do that?"

"With his smartphone."

"When did he get that?"

"I don't know. He's in your class. You should ask him."

I guess it didn't matter when Kyle got his smartphone. The important part was that he used it. On us.

"So Kyle has a video of our dancing?"

"Video of our dancing? Yay!" Kavita said.

"Quiet," I said to Kavita as I tried to listen to Megan.

"Did you all dance? We only saw you."

"Oh!"

I wished Kyle had taken a video of Kavita's or Jay's
dance and not mine. Megan said something else too,
but I didn't hear her. It didn't matter. How did I get
myself in such trouble? How was it that when Kavita
and Jay danced, the school bus didn't pass by?

Lucky dancing was my bad luck.

"Nina, I have to go and start packing for our trip,"
Megan said.

"Have fun in California."

"Thanks. Good luck on your project," she said.

But how could I work on my project when I had a
brand new worry?

My new worry was: Half of the school, well maybe not half, but an entire busload of kids had watched my sidewalk dance performance. Kyle had video of it. For sure, Kyle and the others will talk to the rest of the school. How was I going to face the whole school? Too bad I only knew magic to convert Granny Smith to Pink Lady for Kavita but didn't know a disappearing magic.

So now I had to come up with some kind of a plan. As soon as I finished my Pink Lady, I made a list of ideas for how to avoid any more embarrassment.

Em-bar-rass-ment means something you do or say that makes you wish you were someone else.

How to avoid embarrassment list

* Deny that I was dancing. (But that wouldn't work because Kyle had taken the video.)

* Snatch Kyle's phone and delete the video. (Taking something that wasn't mine was wrong, so this wasn't an option.)

* Change my school. (Mom and Dad would not go for that.)

* Wear a mask to school. But Halloween was still seven months away.

* Spring break might make everyone forget my sidewalk dancing. (That was a possibility.) If not, just ignore the whole school.

For the rest of my life.

CHAPTER FIVE

On Saturday morning, I slept late and had a brunch of aloo paratha. I peeled potatoes, then added salt, lemon, fresh cilantro, and ginger. I made small balls out of the mixture and Mom stuffed each one in a dough disk and rolled it out. Then she cooked them. Kavita ate her aloo paratha plain, Mom and Dad ate theirs with spicy pickles, and I ate mine with ketchup.

Kavita and Dad cleaned up and I helped Mom order seeds from various catalogs. Then Mom had to work.

"Can we go to Picnic Point?" I asked Dad. There are five lakes in Madison, Wisconsin, where I live. Picnic Point is on Lake Mendota. "We can take bhel puri for a snack." Bhel puri is my favorite food—a mix of crunchy chickpea noodles, puffed rice, and bits of sour green mango and ruby red pomegranate seeds, drizzled with sweet-and-sour chutney. To me, it tastes like India. All mixed-up and delicious. And it is something I want to have even when I'm not very hungry.

Dad was on the couch sipping his ginger chai. "It's too windy to be out on the lake," he said.

"How about Olbrich Gardens?" The gardens are across another lake, Lake Monona.

He pointed to the rushing dark clouds. "It looks like it might rain."

Just then the drops started to hit the window. *Plip-plop, plip-plop* at first, then *plip-plippty-plop-plip-plippty-plop*, and finally so fast that all the *plips, plops,* and *plipptys* became one big sound.

Dad looked like he was ready for a nap.

"Then how about the Children's Museum?" I asked before he could fall asleep with a mug of chai in his hand.

Dad shook his head slowly and said, "I have a terrible headache." He placed his half-finished drink on the table and closed his eyes.

He must have had a bad headache, because he always finishes his chai. Then he sneezed. Maybe he was getting a head cold.

Mom was cooped up in her office drawing plans for someone's yard. Spring, summer, and fall are her busy times because she is a landscape architect and master gardener. That means she not only draws plans for people's yards, but also scoops the soil from here to there, places stones and statues, installs fences and plants trees, shrubs, and flowers to make yards look pretty. That also means she doesn't have much time to be out and about with us.

Mom was busy, Dad had a headache. Jay was spending the weekend with his cousins, Nora and Jeff, in Chicago. Megan was on vacation at a beach in California. And all I had was my sister-fixer project today.

Not fair.

I went to my room and sat in my chair holding Lucky. Sakhi was on the desk. That was a good sign.

I made a list.

* Kavita was available.

* The sooner I fixed her, the sooner I could start writing *Five Easy Steps to Fix a Sister (FESTFAS).*

* And I had less than three days left (because today I had already taken time to sleep, cook, and eat) before we went to the cabin with Jay and his family.

* What could I do with Kavita to make her stop singing?

Lucky and I looked out the window and observed. There was a lot of stuff going on out there, so Lucky and I had to make another list.

Our looking-out-the-window observation list

* It had stopped raining, but there were still black clouds hanging around.
* The trees were dripping water.
* The grass was wet.
* Even the rabbits and squirrels were hiding.
* Water was flowing in the gutter by our neighbor's house.
* The big mud pile in their driveway was covered with a tarp.

"Lucky, what would you do with Kavita on a day like this?" I asked.

Lucky didn't answer, but I knew what he would do. He would build a dam!

Then I had a brilliant thought. If Kavita and I built a dam, we could spend a lot of time together. I could work on her as well as the dam. And if she got interested in dam building, she might forget about singing.

On top of that, we could observe if the dam stopped water from going into the gutter. Would it create a puddle? Maybe I could call it Lake Nina. (Puddle Nina didn't sound as good as Lake Nina, so I decided to imagine the puddle as a lake.) Maybe Kavita wanted a lake named after her also. We could combine our names and call it Lake Ninita. But if we wanted a lake named after us, we had to build a dam right away. Before more rain fell.

I was going to get two projects done at the same time! Fix Kavita and build a dam.

It was as good as getting two scoops of ice cream in one cone.

I put Lucky down for a nap, closed Sakhi, and went downstairs.

Kavita was making beds for her dolls from pieces of an old sari Mom had given her. "Come on, Kavita. Let's go out."

I pulled on my rain boots and grabbed my windbreaker.

Sometimes I don't want Kavita tagging along, but this was different. Today she was indispensable.

In-dis-pens-able means something you really need.

I really really needed Kavita.

"But it's raining," she said.

"It's just drizzling. Drizzle-fun is awesome."

She sprang up. "Okay."

She was probably bored. How fun can it be making doll beds? I hate making even my own bed because you make it in the morning and the same night you have to mess it up. Once I tried to sleep without messing it up. I slept on top of my quilt and bedspread, and then in the middle of the night, I was so cold that I had to mess up my bed to get warm.

"Can you help me with my jacket?" Kavita asked.

"Dad, we're going outside. We'll stay close to the house," I said as soon as I zipped Kavita's jacket.

He waved us off. "Okay. Stay safe and don't get into any trouble."

"We will. I mean, we won't. You know, get in trouble. I mean, not get in trouble." Sometimes I trip on my own thoughts and words. If I try to explain more, I trip even more. So I added, "And I'll take good care of Kavita."

Even though Dad had a terrible headache, he gave me an I-am-happy-with-you smile. "You're a great sister."

I nodded because most of the time I'm a good sister. Sometimes I am even a great sister.

"*Trouble, trouble, they bubble, out of our magical cauldron. If you want trouble, come to us and we will dish out some,*" Kavita sang as I closed the door.

My Kavita project had already started. At least her part had.

I thought of my list. I started with the first one.

"Kavita, If you sing your throat might hurt." I touched my throat to show her what I meant.

"My throat is used to singing. It likes it." She put her chin all the way down and asked herself, "Don't you, throat?"

"Why do you sing made-up songs?"

"Aren't all songs made-up by someone?" she said.

"I suppose."

She started to sing again.

Now my part of being embarrassed was almost there. I put my palm over her mouth. "Shhhh! The neighbors can hear you. It might even hurt their ears."

She wiggled herself away. "The Gateses' car is not in the driveway, so they're gone."

I pointed to the house on the other side. "But the Crumps will hear."

"No, they won't. They're gone to their cabin. I spied on them yesterday. They packed their van with lots of stuff. I was so close that I even heard what Mrs. Crump said to Mr. Crump."

"What did she say?"

Kavita stood with her feet apart, scrunched up her face, and folded her arms in the front like Mrs. Crump does. "George, when we get to the cabin, you have to trim the crab apple. If you don't, that branch, you know which one I'm talking about, is going to be the death of my new van."

Kavita had heard Mrs. Crump.

Mr. and Mrs. Crump have a cabin up north, so I guess they're gone. They are always working on a project. When the weather is nice, they do garden projects, and when it is cold, they do inside projects. Lately they'd been building a big round flower bed and filling it up with dirt. But this weekend they were gone. Maybe that's why they covered the pile of dirt in their driveway. To protect it from rain.

"What drizzle-fun are we going to have?" Kavita asked.

Maybe building a dam was the activity to make her forget about singing.

"You know beavers build dams. So just like Lucky, we're going to build a dam."

"Oh yes. I love amazing dams!" Then she asked, "What are they?"

CHAPTER SIX

I explained to Kavita. "A dam stops water from flowing away. That way you can use it." I pointed to the water flowing into the storm sewer in front of the Crumps' house. "We will build a dam right here so the rainwater doesn't drain away. And then we will have a lake. Lake Ninita."

She sang, "*We are going to build a dam. A dam will make a lake, a lake full of rainwater. Water to splash, water to swim, and water to...to do something.*"

Again, it was my chance to stop Kavita singing,

but I also needed to work on our dam. So I ignored her singing.

While Kavita sang, I looked around for dam-building materials.

* There was a pile of dirt in the Crumps' driveway, but it wasn't ours.
* There were soggy leaves. They were smelly.
* There were a few sticks, but not enough of them.
* I needed something strong, like driveway strong. A lot of it. Concrete?

Even though there were cracks in our driveway, it didn't seem easy to dig up. Plus, Dad wouldn't be happy if we dug up our driveway to build a dam.

Suddenly I remembered something I learned when I first got Lucky. Beavers build dams using mud mixed with sticks, stones, leaves, and whatever other stuff they find. Just like beavers, I could add soggy leaves, sticks, and small stones to mud.

It would be like making an awesome beaver-like dam.

Lucky would be proud of me.

I ran into the garage to get the garden trowels—a small plastic one for Kavita and a real metal one for me. I glanced at our neighbors' huge pile of dirt. It wasn't ours.

Instead we started digging by our mailbox. Mom and Dad probably wouldn't mind that because no grass was growing there.

It was time to get back to my second project too. "Kavita, why do you make up songs?" I asked.

"Because it's fun."

"OK. But you know, even if you make them up, you don't need to sing them."

"What's the use of making up songs if you don't

sing them? It's like building a dam and not having any water in it."

It took me a while but finally I dug up a trowel full of mud. It would be nice if I could come up with a trowel full of ideas to fix my sister's singing. "But you don't need to sing them loudly or in front of other people, right?"

She waved her yellow plastic trowel. "Why not? The singers do that all the time. Right?"

"I guess so," I said.

I should have been better prepared. What more could I say to convince Kavita? The list I had made was not working and I needed new ideas. Usually my head is full of tracks and ideas run this way and that way on them. Today they were on strike, so the tracks were bare.

"This is not fun," Kavita said. "Look at my pile. It's shorter than an anthill."

Her pile *was* small. I looked at my pile. It was three

times as big as Kavita's. Maybe as tall as an anthill, but very short for a dam. I shook my head. "I don't know what else we could use. Mud is the best thing."

Kavita handed me her trowel. "I'm going in."

"Wait, wait," I said. Neither of my projects were working out. "Let me think." I had to come up with something quick before she went in and started making doll beds again. Even though I tried not to set my attention on our neighbor's yard, my eyes rested on the pile of dirt in the Crumps' driveway and refused to move. My eyes helped my head make a list.

In-my-head list of why we should use the Crumps' dirt
✳ Mud was the perfect material for a dam.
✳ The dirt pile was huge.
✳ It would be easy to scoop from it.
✳ It was not ours, but it wasn't total strangers' either.

* We borrowed things from each other sometimes. (When Mrs. Crump had a cold, Mom gave her turmeric to take with honey. Mrs. Crump gave us a platter of fresh cookies every time she baked.)
* Now they had a fresh pile of dirt. They wouldn't mind sharing some with us.

"Let's use some of the dirt from Mr. and Mrs. Crump's pile," I said to Kavita. "We can mix it with sticks, leaves, stones, and rainwater and *jadu manter, choo manter*, it will turn into dam-building material."

Kavita's eyes widened. "Won't Mr. and Mrs. Crump grumble?"

"They have a huge pile. So if we borrow very little of it, they won't mind. Plus, the dam will be in front of their house, so it's okay to use their dirt. Their house, their mud, right?"

"Right," Kavita said. She ran into the garage and came back with a purple beach pail.

I rolled out my red wheelbarrow.

The mound was covered with a tarp, held down by a few bricks on the sides. Still, there was enough room to stick in our shovels and get out some dirt.

"This is so amazing!" Kavita said. She had just learned the word amazing and she used it like it was free. Which I suppose it was, but even a free thing can get to be too much. "We should always have a dirt pile to dig in."

"Or make sure one of our neighbors does."

Once my wheelbarrow and Kavita's pail were full, we carried them to the storm sewer.

The water was still flowing, so it didn't take any time to make mud. We added leaves and sticks and a few small stones to the dirt and built a wall around the storm sewer. It was high enough that the water stopped going in.

All through the dam making, Kavita was not sing-ing. Keeping her busy with a challenging project was good. I figured she just needed to be interested in something else to get the songs and singing out of her mind.

"Instead of singing, how about if you draw, paint, and color? You're good at art. You can have your own art show," I said as I slapped more mud around the storm sewer.

"I can sing and draw at the same time," Kavita said.

She was missing my point. "It's better to pay attention to one thing at a time. Right?"

Kavita didn't answer.

I went to fill up the wheelbarrow again. As I was coming back, I spied dark clouds. Oh no, the drizzle was going to turn into real rain soon.

"Kavita, let's be quick and make the other walls so we can have a lake."

There was no Kavita. Where did she go?

I sprinted all the way around the house. "Kavita? Kavita? KAVITA?"

No answer.

She was not in the side yard or in the back. Where was she? Maybe I should go in and tell Mom and Dad.

But luckily I didn't need to do that, because when I got back, Kavita was standing by the dam.

"There you are," she said, sprinkling something from a bowl.

"And here you are," I said huffing and puffing, but not so hard as to blow away my dam.

Kavita sang, *"Dam, build a great big dam. A dam full of rainwater to splash and swim in. Rainwater to plant rice in."*

"Plant rice? Is that what you're doing?" I asked.

I guess she had not taken my advice. Her song making and singing at the top of her lungs were still going strong.

"Yes, like we've seen in pictures. Remember those women wearing saris standing in water to plant rice?"

"They were harvesting rice. Not planting, I think."

"But they must have planted it before. How could they harvest it if they never planted it?"

As Dad would say, she had a point. "I guess so."

Kavita offered me the bowl, but not before scooping up a handful. "Here, you plant some."

She sprinkled rice on the mud, singing, *"Grow, grow, grow your rice, gently toward the sky. Merrily, merrily, merrily, merrily, life is but a green."*

So now the mud was specked with organic white and brown rice, and Lake Ninita was contaminated with rice too.

Con-tam-i-nate means a thing you don't want shows up in something. Like if red paint gets contaminated with yellow paint.

I didn't especially want rice to show up in my lake. I also knew it wasn't going to grow there because the lake was going to fill up with water, so it didn't matter. I sprinkled the rice too.

Just as we were done planting, the rain began to *plip-plop* again. Then it began to come down faster than *plip-plop*. We grabbed the wheelbarrow and the pail. We dropped them in the garage. Once we got inside the house, we took off our muddy boots and jackets and washed our hands.

Kavita went back to making doll beds.

I watched the rain from the window. It was hard to see how much lake was filling up in front of Mr. and Mrs. Crump's house.

"Did you have fun outside?" Dad asked.

"We did."

Because of his headache, he didn't ask more questions.

And I didn't volunteer any more information.

Vol-un-teer means give something without anyone asking and for free.

Dad had not asked what exactly we were doing. Since his head was full of ache, there was probably no room for information.

So I didn't mention our dam. It was in the Crumps' yard, built with their dirt.

A little voice in my head said, *But it was our dam, our lake. We shouldn't have taken the dirt from our neighbor's pile to build it.*

I pretended not to hear that little voice.

CHAPTER SEVEN

On Sunday morning, the rain whispered, *rim-zim,*
rim-zim. Kavita was hunched over the dining table
with crayons and markers and a packet of colorful
paper.

She had taken my advice and was drawing and
coloring. Yay!

"What are you making?" I asked.

"It's a secret," she said. "How do you spell 'happy'?"

So I spelled "h-a-p-p-y." She wrote it down. She
asked the spelling for another word.

I said, "*s-p-r-i-n-g.*" She was probably writing a

song. Before she could ask me how to spell an entire poem, I walked into the living room.

Dad stood by the window, gazing out. I stood by him and looked up. His face was all scrunched up like a crumpled piece of paper.

"What are you looking at, Dad?"

He squinted. "A small puddle. The rainwater is certainly slow to drain."

Lake Ninita! I screamed inside my head. Screaming inside your head is okay because no one hears it and asks you to be quiet. I had to go out and check.

I glanced into the dining room at Kavita.

She was still bent over her secret project, probably writing down not-so-secret words. Yesterday when we built the dam, I took Kavita with me, but today I didn't want her along.

The reasons I didn't want Kavita to go with me were many

* Kavita was drawing and coloring. I didn't want to disturb her.
* It had replaced her singing. That's what I had hoped would happen.
* She might get upset if all the rice we planted yesterday had floated away.
* If the dam was working, she might make up a song for it.
* She might sing it loud and clear.
* It might make Mom and Dad check the puddle.

✳ They might sweep it away before the lake had a chance to fully form.

"Kavita is busy with her secret project, so I will go by myself to investigate," I whispered to Dad.

> To *in-ves-ti-gate* means to find out more about something. It is as if there is a gate that you go through and see what is happening.

Dad nodded.

"What are you doing?" he asked Kavita.

Didn't I just tell him that Kavita was working on a secret project? Sometimes Dad's hearing is not very good. Maybe I can work on a hearing aid for him. That could be *my* secret project.

"I'm making cards for Jay and his family," Kavita replied. So much for her "secret" project.

"That is so nice of you. Make sure you make one for each of them," I encouraged Kavita.

> To **en-cour-age** means to give courage to someone about something they want to do or are trying to do. That way they don't quit.

While Kavita was still full of my encouragement, I asked Dad if I could borrow his phone.

"Why?"

"There might be something interesting out there."

He handed me the phone. "Make sure it doesn't get wet."

"I will."

I pulled on my rain boots and zipped up my raincoat. I slipped the phone in my pocket. As soon as I closed the door, I dashed to the side of the house. Then stopped.

Wow!

The gutter in front of the Crumps' curb was a puddle, all right.

I waded in the water to get a closer look. The mud-stick-leaves mixture still surrounded the gutter. The white and brown specks were still there. Who knows, maybe we would get some rice sprouting too.

If I took a picture Dad would see it right away. Then he might ask questions. I wanted my puddle to have time to get bigger.

A selfie would cover most of the pond.

One, two, three, press.

A mosquito headed straight at me!

I tried to swat it away.

It escaped. Then buzzed in my ear. I swiped at it. Again, it escaped but I did not.

I lost my balance.

Splash!

Right into the pond.

Still, I was able to keep my phone-holding hand up so the phone didn't get ruined. And I saved my selfie! I walked back to the house *drip-dripping* with muddy water. Also, I suppose, with some rice sticking to my rain boots.

I rushed into the laundry room and peeled off my raincoat and boots as fast as I could.

"Did you take pictures?" Dad asked when I handed him the phone.

"Only one. The water—"

Oops, I almost spilled the beans—I mean the rice.

"The water? What's the problem?" His eyes focused on the picture.

"No problem. You were right, Dad. The water behind me is slow to drain. That's all."

Which was the truth. The water was slow to drain...because Kavita and I had piled mud on the storm sewer, but I didn't mention the mud-piling part. I wanted Dad and Mom to be impressed by my project. Maybe some more rain would make the puddle bigger. If the puddle was bigger, they wouldn't have to use too much imagination to make it into a lake.

I was happy as I took a good-scrubbing shower.

My sister-fixer project and the dam project were both working!

Kavita was coloring.

Our dam had made a puddle.

And that puddle + imagination = Lake Ninita.

(I used my imagination and stretched it into a lake. Because a lake is a puddle first and then it gets bigger and bigger.)

> Usually 1 + 1 = 2, but imagination is like 1 + infinity. It could be anything.

After my shower I was all set to work on Kavita while the rain made the puddle larger.

"Still working on your secret project, Kavita?" I asked.

Kavita held up the cards. "Yup. I have made eight cards so far."

"Can I look at them?"

"No!" she said. "It's a surprise."

"But I already know you're making cards and they aren't for me. So why can't I see them?"

"It's still a surprise. When they open them at their cabin, I want you to be surprised too. They're going to be amazing."

Now I had no choice but to wait until we went to the cabin to find out what was in the cards.

I crossed my fingers, hoping Kavita wasn't writing down made-up songs that would embarrass me.

CHAPTER EiGHT

All afternoon it rained like the clouds were turning their faucets on and off just for fun. Kavita had a birthday party to go to. I stayed in my room, working on fractions and watching my lake. My window was the best place to watch the Crumps' yard because it opens to their side of our house. Plus, our house is much higher, so I could see everything in their front yard. The storm sewer area had filled up, so it wouldn't be long before Lake Ninita spread. It made me happy.

In the evening I could see a reflection of the street-light in Lake Ninita. Even a part of the sidewalk was underwater. What if the Crumps' house drowned in Lake Ninita?

Oh no!

Maybe the dam had not been a great idea.

Not on our street.

Not by our neighbors' house.

Not with so much rain.

I prayed for the rain to stop, but the sky, the clouds, the rain, or the Rain God were not listening to my prayers. Maybe they also needed hearing aids.

On top of that, my stomach began to hurt. It was as if it was full of grains of rice and they were all sprouting.

I found Mom in the kitchen, cleaning the counters.

"Mom, my stomach hurts."

"Take some ajvan seeds," Kavita said. "Let me get them for you."

"That is very nice of you, Kavita," Mom said.

I swallowed the tiny seeds Kavita gave me with sips of water and went to the living room.

Mom came in the room. "How do you feel?"

"A little better."

"Maybe you ate too fast. If you want, get ready for bed. Then read a book," she said. "I'm also exhausted. It will be good for all of us to get some rest."

I said good night, went up, brushed my teeth, and changed into my pj's. I read in bed until I got sleepy. Just when I switched off my table lamp, *crash!* A big streak of lightning slashed the sky. Thunder followed.

More rain, bigger puddle, bigger problem, I thought. Worries burrowed in my head and trickled down to my stomach. My rice-paddy stomach now felt full of worry and ajvan plants all getting tangled up. It began to hurt again.

I went looking for Mom and Dad. It was dark downstairs. Maybe because of Dad's headache and Mom's exhaustion, they had gone to bed early.

Ex-haus-tion means you're very tired and need rest.

What I could do

* Take ajvan seeds.

* But I had already taken them.

* Wake up Mom or Dad.

* But they needed rest.

* And they might take me to the emergency.

* My stomach wasn't hurting emergency-bad.

But there was something else I could do! I could ask my grandmother. She was in India, but I could call her. Night in the USA meant it was day in India.

I went down to the kitchen and called Dadi's cell phone. It rang and rang but she didn't answer. So I called the home number. My cousin Montu answered.

"Where is Dadi?" I asked. I whispered because I didn't want to wake anyone up.

Montu is seven, smack between Kavita's and my ages. My dadi is his dadi, too, and they live together in the same house.

"Everyone has gone to a wedding except Dada and me."

"At nine in the morning?"

"They went yesterday. It's in Delhi."

"Oh." I wondered if Dada would know what to do.

"You sound *bhago*," Montu said.

"What is *bhago*?"

"That's my own word. It means miserable. Like you have swallowed Dadi's bitter medicine."

"What bitter medicine?" I didn't know anything about that.

"The one she gives in monsoon. Never mind. You don't have monsoons there."

"We do. Right now."

"Even in monsoon you don't have to take the medicine because Dadi is not there to give it to you. Luck-ee!"

Okay. I didn't know why we were discussing bitter-monsoon medicine and not stomach medicine.

"I need to ask Dadi what to do for my stomach-ache. I'll call her again."

"She won't hear you."

Indian weddings are superlong and supernoisy. "Is she at an Indian wedding?" I asked.

"No, a Japanese wedding!" Then he added, "Of course, it is in India so it is an Indian wedding. Don't worry though, I think I know what to do."

I waited while my stomach was dying. This was not helping.

"Montu? Are you there?"

"Yes." Montu sounded annoyed. "I remember! When I fell on the playground and had pain, Dadi put a paste of turmeric and salt on my leg. Worked really well. Rub that on your tummy."

Rub turmeric and salt on my stomach? Was he crazy?

"But I didn't fall. I just have a stomachache."

"Dadi says turmeric takes pain away. It really

works. You should even eat some turmeric just so you have turmeric on the inside and outside of your stomach."

Great. "Okay, thanks. Bye."

"Hey, don't hang up. Talk to me."

"I have to go, Montu. Remember, I have to make turmeric paste to put on my stomach."

"Oh, okay." He sounded unhappy. "If you or Kavita need help, just call me."

"Sure."

I called Dadi's cell phone again. She still didn't answer.

I wasn't sure if Montu knew what he was talking about. Maybe I should wait for Dadi to call me back. But she might not call until tomorrow. By that time my stomach had better be better. I needed something. Now.

I thought:

* Mom uses turmeric in cooking and also mixes it with honey when I have a sore throat. (Even when Mrs. Crump had a cold, Mom gave her turmeric to take with honey.)
* It makes my sore throat feel better.
* Dadi put turmeric on Montu when he fell.
* It helped him feel better.
* A pain is pain—throat, leg, or stomach. And we eat turmeric every day so it should be safe to apply it to my stomach.

We have a stainless-steel box filled with spices we use all the time. There are many containers in it filled with red, brown, and yellow powders and black and orangey-yellow seeds. Turmeric is the bright yellow powder.

I mixed turmeric with sea salt and added water. It was just like mixing dirt and water to make mud.

You don't add too much water, just enough to make a paste. I took it to the bathroom. I know very well how it stains, so I was careful not to get it on the floor or sink.

I lifted up my pj's and rubbed turmeric over my stomach. I even filled my belly button with the bright yellow paste.

I stayed in the bathroom until the paste kind of dried, which didn't take too long, and then pulled my shirt back down.

When I came out of the bathroom, Dad was there. So was Kavita.

I was surprised. "I thought everyone was asleep."

"Mom is asleep. I was telling stories to Kavita," Dad said. "We heard the bathroom door so we came down. Are you okay?"

"No. My stomach hurts. Please don't ask me to take ajvan seeds. I already did."

"Oh!"

I waited for him to tell me to apply turmeric, but he did not. Maybe Dad didn't know about it. He took off his glasses. "Let's wake up Mom. Maybe we need to go to the emergency." He looked worried.

"Is it serious?" Kavita asked.

"Not very serious," I said.

Kavita ran out of the room. Probably to wake up Mom.

"Does it hurt in one spot or all over?" Dad asked.

"All over. Mom said it's probably because I ate dinner too fast."

"Come, let's go to the couch. Lie down on your left side and you might feel better. I'll get you a pillow and a blanket."

After I lay down, Dad rubbed my back gently. I felt better. Maybe it was the turmeric or Dad's rubbing, but something was working.

"How are you doing, Nina?" Dad asked.

I smiled. "Better."

Someone rang the doorbell. Dad rushed to open the door.

"Meera?"

Jay's mom was standing outside holding an umbrella. Oh no, it was still raining.

Just then Mom came down the stairs. She must have heard the doorbell. "What is going on?"

"Kavita called to say something serious has happened. Not *very* serious, but serious," Meera Masi said.

"Kavita called?" Dad asked.

Didn't Meera Masi just say that? I must work on that hearing aid soon.

Kavita came in clutching a phone. "Nina has a stomachache."

"I told you it wasn't serious," I said.

"You said it wasn't *very* serious. That means it is still serious. And Mom says we have to call Meera Masi if something is serious."

"Only if Mom and Dad are not around or something happens to them," I said. Nobody was listening to me.

"What happened? Nina, are you hurt?" Mom asked. Her hair was sticking in every direction. Mom was not having a good hair night.

"Nina has a stomachache, but she is feeling better," Dad said. Then he bent over and added, "Kavita, next time ask before you call Meera Masi, okay?"

"But you said you wanted to take Nina to the emergency. And you always tell me to call 911 if there is an emergency."

Dad eyes widened. "You didn't call 911? Did you?"

"Yes. I even told them our address—They are on the phone."

Dad grabbed the phone and explained to the person on the other end what had happened.

Mom sat down next to me. "Where does it hurt?" she asked while Dad was still explaining to the 911 person.

I grabbed my shirt tightly and pulled it down. "It doesn't hurt much. I'm fine. Really, I am."

Meera Masi sat on my other side. "Show us where it hurts."

Great. I was sandwiched between my mom and Jay's mom.

Didn't I say I was fine? But now Mom and Meera Masi were not going to let me leave the couch before I showed them where it hurt. I pointed at the middle of my stomach. "Right around here." I clutched my shirt as Mom felt my stomach.

"Why is your shirt stained kind of yellow?" Jay asked.

When had he snuck in? Why didn't this happen yesterday, when he was in Chicago?

I could have drowned in my own embarrassment. I closed my eyes to fight the tears that prickled my eyes. They might soak my shirt and then everyone would for sure see my yellow stomach.

"Why is it yellow?" Mom asked.

Great and double great. Now I had to answer.

"Montu told me to rub turmeric paste on my stomach," I said, opening my eyes.

Mom shook her head. "Montu? You talked to Montu about it?"

"Is Montu her doctor?" Jay asked. Even though he should have remembered that Montu is my cousin.

"Montu is seven." Dad's voice was bitter, as if it was Montu's fault that he was only seven. Dad turned to me. "Since when is Montu your doctor?"

I wished he was still talking to the 911 person.

"Oh, your cousin Montu!" Jay said.

Did Jay think it was possible to know more than one person named Montu?

"Quiet, Jay," Meera Masi said.

Kavita sang, *"Montu, Montu, I have a cousin named Montu. What more can you ask, when you have a cousin named Montu?"*

Kavita's singing reminded me that my sister-fixer project had run into a problem. I mean, she was singing at the most awkward time of my life.

Dad looked at Kavita. "That's enough singing."

I guess Dad was taking over my job, or at least helping me out.

Meera Masi grabbed Jay's hand. "Let's go home."

But before they left, Jay looked back and whispered, "Turmeric on your tummy?"

I gave him a look that said *don't even think about mentioning this at school.* He smirked. Then he and Meera Masi left and I felt sick all over again. This was because

* I had taken seven-year-old Montu's advice.
* I had rubbed turmeric on my stomach.
* My stomach was bright yellow and would stay that way for days.
* Jay knew about it.
* Our dam was working.
* And the puddle was changing to Lake Ninita.
* It could get very big.
* I should tell Mom and Dad about it.
* But I didn't know how.

Before I could figure out what to say to my parents and how to say it, Dad took Kavita to her room to tuck her back in.

"Let me get you some water," Mom said to me. "You might be dehydrated." She went to the kitchen.

While they were gone, the front door opened and Jay peeked in. "Just grabbing Mom's umbrella," he said. Then he looked around and whispered, "Neon yellow stomach! A new fashion?"

As if I had done it on purpose!

As soon as he left, Mom walked in with a glass of water.

I took a few sips and was feeling much better when Dad returned.

I saw out the window that the rain had stopped. No need to say anything to them now. Plus, I still didn't know what to say or how to say it.

Maybe a good night's sleep would help my brain work better tomorrow.

CHAPTER NiNE

When Kavita saw me Monday morning, her greeting was "Is your stomach still yellow?"

I wanted to say no, but that would be lying. So I didn't answer. It was still yellow and would stay that way for a few more days. I knew that because when Mom cuts fresh turmeric, she wears gloves to avoid having yellow fingers for a week. There wasn't anything I could do to make my stomach nonyellow, non-neon any sooner.

The sun was shining and my plan was to go out and check Lake Ninita.

Maybe I could peek at it from the living room window first. I walked in.

I knew Mom and Dad were discussing something serious because their faces wore frowns.

"It looks like we got a ton of rain," Dad said.

Mom pointed at the Crumps' front yard. "I wonder what's blocking the storm sewers."

My rice-paddy neon yellow stomach began to sprout worries again. Along with ajvan seeds.

Dad squinted as he looked out. "I can't tell."

"The water is almost as high as the retaining wall." Mom sounded panicked.

I guessed they were talking about Lake Ninita. Of course, they didn't call it Lake Ninita.

"What will happen, Mom?" I asked.

"If the rain from yesterday keeps draining toward the storm sewer but can't get down it, the water will flow over the wall. Especially if we get more rain."

Mom was right. The water was so high that if it

rained any more, it was going to flow over the retaining wall like a waterfall.

First a lake. Then a waterfall. Wow!

"Let's go out and check. Maybe there's something we can do," Mom said, "before the wall crumbles and their basement gets ruined."

"What will get ruined?" Kavita asked as she walked into the room.

"The retaining wall," I answered and quickly moved between Kavita and the window so she couldn't see Lake Ninita. But she ducked around me.

"Nina!" She clapped. "Lookee-look-look. Our amazing dam is working! Maybe our rice is growing too."

Kavita had spilled our rice.

Mom and Dad looked at me as if they were shocked and worried at the same time.

They knew!

There was no way to make them not know. I had

deeper worries than my yellow stomach. Because now my heart seemed to sink down to my stomach.

"Is that what you were doing the other afternoon?" Dad asked.

"Dad, Mom," I tried to explain but all the tracks of my mind were empty.

"Where did you get the materials to build a dam?" Dad asked.

"There's a pile of dirt in the Crumps' driveway, so we used it to try and make a dam. I didn't think it would work. But it did and I was afraid to say anything. I'm sorry."

"We'll talk about it later. Let's fix the problem first," Mom said.

The next thing I knew I was out with Mom, Dad, and Kavita with our wheelbarrow and shovels. We moved a mixture of dirt, sticks, and soggy leaves—well, the soggy leaves didn't look like leaves anymore.

The wet mud-stick-leaves mixture was heavy. Kavita's plastic shovel didn't work at all. I could only get a little bit out at a time. Mom and Dad did most of the work. We piled the mixture in the wheelbarrow. Not only did I have a hard time, but Mom's face was red and Dad had perspiration on his forehead.

Even Kavita must have known this was serious, because she was not making up songs about broken dams.

Lucky and other beavers are lucky they only have to build dams, not break them.

As we cleared the mud and the dam broke, the water gushed toward the storm sewer.

I gasped. That was it. That was the end of Lake Ninita and all the rice.

We watched Lake Ninita disappear down the storm sewer.

I had this great idea to build a dam. Kavita and I had worked on it. It had held the water back and almost created a lake. Our almost-own-Lake-Ninita! Now there was nothing of our project left except a pile of mud-stick-leaves in the wheelbarrow.

I felt achy. Not in my stomach, but in my heart. Like my heart was draining.

Mom looked up. Her face looked tired. "Finally, it's draining well."

Kavita held up her plastic shovel. "It broke."

"Sorry," I whispered.

"It's not your fault," she said. "I'm hungry. Can we have some snack?"

"Sure," Dad said. "Let's go in. I'll empty the wheelbarrow later."

"Can I stay out?" I asked, staring down at the storm sewer.

"Are you going to build another dam?" Kavita asked.

I shook my head.

Mom and Dad glanced at each other.

"No. I just want to—I want to stay." I turned away so they wouldn't see my tears.

"Don't try to bring the wheelbarrow in by yourself. It's very heavy," Mom said. "We'll bring it in later, after the mud dries out. "

"Okay." My voice was as small as I felt.

"And when you come in, we have to talk," Mom said.

I guessed just taking down the dam and letting Lake Ninita drain out was not enough. There was more for me to do. Like explain more...and say I was sorry. I didn't know how I was going to do it. I was scared and worried.

"Sure," I whispered. But I wasn't sure at all.

After the three of them went in, I stayed outside watching the last rice whirling in the water of Lake Ninita as it flowed down the storm sewer. It made me sad. My dam experiment had worked, but I had almost flooded the Crumps' basement.

Unfortunately if you are a kid, sometimes the most important thing is not your brilliant idea, but getting permission from your parents. To make sure it is safe to put your ideas into action.

I had forgotten that rule.

On top of that, I had tried to hide my dam from Mom and Dad. I really wanted to see if it worked. Deep down I knew they would tell me to take it down so the water could flow freely. And I had not thought through the problems a dam could cause.

And I was so caught up in it that I had even abandoned my first project of sister fixing.

A-ban-don means to give up.

I had no dam, I hadn't fixed my sister, and I was in trouble with Mom and Dad. What should I do? I wondered.

* Go to Meera Masi's house?
* But then I would have to explain what had happened.
* And Jay would find out about my dam and the big flood I almost caused.

* I knew it was better to go into my own
  house and be brave.
* Yes, I was going to be brave.

Before I had a chance to be brave, the Crumps
came home. But they didn't drive straight to their
driveway and into their garage. They stopped by the
curb and Mr. Crump got out. He stared at the last few
drops of Lake Ninita and the pile of mud mixture in
the wheelbarrow.

"What happened here?" He looked at my shovel
and added, "What are you doing?"

Mrs. Crump rolled down her window.

My courage fled.

"I am...I mean...just cleaning up...just the mud
that was plugging your storm sewer," I said.

Mrs. Crump leaned out the window. "Thank you,
Nina. Mr. Crump must not have covered the dirt pile
well. Without you keeping an eye on our house, this
would have ended in a disaster."

Mr. Crump nodded. "Yes, thank you."

I wanted to tell them about how I had borrowed their mud and built a dam with Kavita's help. But all I said was, "Um...you're welcome. I guess." My own words made me feel terrible. I hadn't lied, but I was hiding something from them.

Mrs. Crump got out of the car, opened the back door, and pulled out a box. "Here, have a cherry pie. We just got several of them from Door County. It was very thoughtful of you to take care of our mud problem."

Should I take it or say no? I thought. Instead of the Crumps getting mad at me, they had given me a cherry pie—but only because I hadn't told them the whole truth.

"Nina?" Mrs. Crump was holding the pie, looking at me. Was she reading my thoughts?

I took the pie. "Thank you."

As I carried the pie in, I wondered if I could convince Mom and Dad that without my dam building, we wouldn't have this cherry pie. If I could, I would be double lucky.

CHAPTER TEN

Double lucky I was not. I handed Mom the cherry pie.

"Where did you get this?" she asked.

When I explained, Mom and Dad didn't smile.

"So you didn't tell the Crumps how you built the dam? From their dirt pile. To cover their storm sewer," Mom said.

Mom was kind of making a list like I do.

"No."

"Let's go over what has happened," Dad said. He always likes to go over stuff. I don't know why we have to go over stuff when it has already happened. And explained once before.

I tried to give them the right introduction first. "You know Lucky Beaver, right?"

"Of course. What about it?" Dad always tells me to be patient with Kavita, but he was not sounding very patient with me.

"Did you know beavers build dams?" I didn't wait for their answers. "I wanted to make a dam like Lucky Beaver. Since it was raining so much, it was the perfect time to build one. When Kavita and I went out, we saw the pile of dirt in the Crumps' driveway. We didn't use it. Not at first. We tried to dig the dirt from our yard, but it was so difficult."

Mom's eyebrows went up when I said we tried to dig dirt from our yard.

"It was by our mailbox where no grass is growing," I quickly added.

"So then you used the Crumps' dirt," Dad said.

I nodded.

Mom lifted my chin and looked straight at me. "Was it right to build a dam without asking?"

Mom knew the answer. Still, I had to reply. "No."

"And you took the dirt from their pile without asking."

"But we weren't *stealing* it. We just moved it by their storm sewer to build a dam. I thought it might turn into a lake."

"It almost did," Dad said.

I glanced at Kavita sitting next to Mom. "Then Kavita wanted to plant rice, so we did that," I finished.

"Rice grows in water, so I wanted to plant it," she said.

"I see," Dad said, looking at Mom.

Mom said one good thing. "We are proud of your creative ideas."

Dad nodded.

I could feel my eyes growing like two round lakes. "You are?"

"Yes, but you must think about your creative ideas and the potential consequences before you act on them," Mom said.

"Yes."

Then everything that was not good came out.

"This could have been a huge disaster," Dad said.

My heart began to shrink like a punctured balloon.

"What is a 'dish-a-stir'?" Kavita asked. "Is it a dish that you stir?"

"No. It means it could have been very bad," Mom replied. "It could have flooded the Crumps' basement. Nina, can you imagine the damage it would have done? Mold would start growing in it and it would cost so much to clean up that mess."

"I'm sorry. Very, very sorry," I said. My voice sounded mushy and limp, like rice soaked in a puddle too long. "I was so excited to build a dam like Lucky. The dam worked and I was happy and proud. In all that, I forgot what damage it might do. Next time I'll act before I think. No, no, I mean I will think before I act."

"The first thing you must do is go up to your room and think about what you did and how you are going to explain to our neighbors. How are you going to tell them you are sorry?" Mom asked.

I didn't have an answer.

"Go up now," Dad said.

When was I supposed to come down? I didn't ask.

I went up to my room and the first thing I did was to hug Lucky. I knew he would understand why I loved building a dam. Then I cried. Sometimes crying is like rain. It helps make everything clear and fresh. When I felt a little clearer and fresher, I made a list in Sakhi. A list of all the things I should have thought about before acting.

* Whether or not plugging a storm sewer was a good idea.

* Whether or not taking dirt from the Crumps' dirt-pile was okay.

* Whether or not it was smart to stay silent about the puddle turning into Lake Ninita.

* Whether or not it was right to hide the truth from Mr. and Mrs. Crump.

After I wrote the list I pondered.

To **pon-der** means to think and think and think about something until it becomes clear.

I realized that plugging the storm sewer was not a good idea because it blocked the water from draining. It flooded the area and it might have damaged the Crumps' basement.

It was definitely not okay to take the dirt from the Crumps' dirt pile without asking them. It was not smart to stay silent. I had made a mistake and by not telling Mom and Dad I was covering it up.

It was also not right to hide the truth from Mr.

and Mrs. Crump. I had taken their dirt, built a dam in front of their house, and almost damaged their house. I had not told them any of it.

Then I took a piece of paper and wrote to my parents.

Dear Mom and Dad,

I am sorry for building a dam and almost flooding our neighbors' yard and basement. I will try to be more responsible in the future. Is it okay if I write a letter to Mr. and Mrs. Crump and tell them everything? Can I come down?

Love you,

Your sorry daughter Nina

P.S. Even if you say I can't come down,

I love you.

I didn't know how I could give the note to Mom and Dad since they were downstairs and I was upstairs.

Usually I would have sent the note down with Kavita, but she didn't come up. Maybe she wasn't allowed to spend time with me. It made me sad on top of being sad. I was a double sad person.

Could I invent a way to send the note down?

I took out the last few tissues from a box and put them on the table. They would come in handy if I caught a cold. Dad had a headache and sneezes, so maybe I would need them soon.

Then I punched holes in the empty box on two sides and strung a string through them. I tied it on the top.

I placed my note in the box and dangled it halfway down the stairs.

I waited and waited.

When Dad came out of the kitchen, I lowered it and almost hit his head with the tissue box. But I stopped just above his head and he disappeared into the living room. He didn't notice something dangling over his head.

So I waited and waited and waited until Mom came out of the room.

I was ready and quick this time, and my box dangled down in front of her face when she came though the hallway.

I jiggled the string and the box danced in front of her. She looked inside and took out my note.

She read it.

I held my breath.

Mom looked up. "Yes," she said. "A letter of apology would work."

I came down and wrote an apology to the Crumps.

An *a-pol-o-gy* means saying you're sorry, but it is longer than just saying I'm sorry. I guess "apology" is a longer word, so it takes longer to apologize than to say sorry.

Here is my apology letter:

Dear Mr. and Mrs. Crump,

While you were gone, I built a dam with the dirt by your curb. (Mr. Crump had covered the dirt pile well.) I even asked Kavita to help me. We also planted some organic brown and white basmati rice. (Those are the best kinds of rice. Have you ever had them?) Anyway, our dam blocked the storm sewer. I am glad nothing bad has happened to your house and yard.

What I did was wrong and I want to apologize for it.

Your neighbor,

Nina

P.S. Should I return the cherry pie?

I took the letter and rang the Crumps' doorbell. Mr. Crump opened the door and Mrs. Crump was right by him. They spend all their time together because they're retired.

> *Re-tired* means you are tired of working and instead spend time doing things you like.

I handed him the letter. "What is it?" Mrs. Crump asked, looking over Mr. Crump's shoulder as he turned the note over in his hand.

I wanted to give them the note and run home, but Mom and Dad had told me that I had to wait until they read it. My heart thumped like I had run up and down our street five times. But all I had done was to walk over to our neighbor's house. My palms were sweaty and my throat was dry. Not a good combination. But I waited.

It sure took them a long time to read because

* They asked me to sit down, which I didn't want to do. (Still, I did it because I wanted to be polite to them.)

* Then they had to find their glasses, which

took them a few minutes. (I guess it is hard to find your glasses when you aren't wearing them and can't see where they are very well.)

They both sat on a couch side by side and read the note.

Once they finished reading, they looked at each other.

Then they looked at me.

Then they read the note again.

By this time, I was sitting on the edge of the chair, ready to bolt home.

"This could have been very bad," Mrs. Crump said, removing her glasses. Her face looked like she had gulped some sour cherry juice.

Mr. Crump took off his glasses and nodded. Since I didn't have glasses on, I just nodded. I hoped that was the polite thing to do.

"Luckily we don't have any water in the basement, so there's no harm done," Mrs. Crump said.

Mr. Crump nodded. I nodded too.

There was a lot of nodding going on. Although it was better than yelling for sure.

But then Mrs. Crump smiled. I couldn't believe my luck. Then Mr. Crump started laughing. Then Mrs. Crump's smile turned into laughter.

* Was I supposed to laugh with them?
* Was I supposed to ask why they were laughing?
* Or could I just go home?

I looked down at my legs and counted the polka dots on my socks. I figured once I counted them all, then I could leave.

"Nina, it's okay," Mrs. Crump said.

"Does that mean you accept my apology?" I asked.

"We certainly do," Mr. Crump said, "as long as you don't build a dam again."

"I never will. I mean, I might become an engineer and build a real dam somewhere, but I won't build one on a street."

I got up to leave but then stopped. "Do you...I mean...Should I bring your pie back?"

"No. You enjoy it," Mrs. Crump said.

"Thank you," I said, and really, really meant it.

＊

That afternoon I stayed in my room and read. Kavita took a nap. Usually she doesn't take naps, but today she must have been tired from dam breaking. Mom and Dad also rested; they were exhausted.

In the evening Dad made curried chickpeas and cauliflower and rice. I made dough with Mom's help. Then Kavita and I rolled rotis.

"Do you think we could take rotis to the cabin tomorrow?" I asked Mom.

"That's a great idea. Jay would enjoy them."

"Look at the one I rolled. It looks like the United States," Kavita said.

"You're supposed to make them round."

"Nina, they all taste the same. And it's fun to make amazing shapes."

Then she burst out singing. *"I love rotis. Round or square, cone or crown, slapped on the skillet, turned over once, then puffed up. Served with ghee, ready, set, chomp."*

On Saturday I had done 1/3 of the job of sister fixing. But yesterday and today I had not worked on stopping my sister's singing. So now 1/3+1/3 = 2/3 of sister fixing was not done.

But come to think of it, Kavita had only made up this one song, about roti, after Dad had told her to be quiet.

"Can you please be amazing and not sing when we are with Jay and his family?" I asked Kavita.

"Maybe," she replied.

I hoped like my turmeric tummy, her singing might fade away by tomorrow.

Just to be sure, I crossed my flour-coated fingers.

CHAPTER ELEVEN

On Tuesday morning the sun woke up bright and bold. I did not.

When I showered, I rubbed my stomach with soap. Then I thought, *Who will see my stomach anyway?* Still, I wore a dark blue shirt so no yellow could be seen. Then I packed my clothes. Kavita's clothes were already in our suitcase, and I stuffed mine on top.

When I went downstairs, the stack of cards Kavita had made was sitting on the dining table. I wanted to open them, but I didn't do that because that wasn't right. I just hoped there was nothing embarrassing in them.

I was ready. Kavita was ready. Dad was making tea. Mom still hadn't showered. "Mom, we're supposed to leave in an hour," I said.

"Yes," she said, reaching for another tissue. She wiped her nose and then closed her eyes. "I feel sick."

"Oh."

If we didn't go to the cabin, what would we do? I wondered.

In-my-head-list of possible stay-at-home activities

* I guess I could work on sister-fixing Kavita.
* But what if she doesn't make up any songs?
* Or doesn't sing them out loud?
* I could just get bored, bored, bored.

Dad brought Mom a pot of tea with honey, ginger, and cinnamon. He sat it on the dining table and the smell traveled from my nose to my head. I felt good without even taking a sip of it. If Mom drank all the tea, I knew she would be okay and we would go.

I looked from Mom to the clock, back to Mom, then out the window. Dad sneezed three times. He also didn't look good.

Kavita opened one of the cards she had made and set it on the table.

"I thought you were done with your cards," I said.

She picked out a crayon from the box. "I have to fix something I missed."

I tried to look over her shoulder. "What did you miss?"

She covered her card with her hands. "If you look, it won't be a surprise."

I turned away. Kavita bent over and worked. She wasn't singing. I hoped the card making had replaced her song making and singing. Forever.

Kavita seemed peaceful, but I didn't feel peaceful.

It was because my mind was whirling. I didn't know if we were going or not. I guess I like planning, and I couldn't plan with Mom feeling sick. On top of that Dad had sneezed like ten times this morning.

After she had her tea, Mom bundled up in her robe and sat on the couch.

"We're not going to the cabin, are we?" I asked.

"I'm achy all over," Mom said.

"Sneezy here," Dad said as if we hadn't noticed it.

Now we were certainly not going. Kavita came in with a pile of cards. "If we can't go I want to give these cards to Jay so he can take them to his family." She looked like she was about to cry.

"Put them in a bag and you and Nina can take them over," Dad said.

"I want to do it by myself," she said. "They're secrets."

The phone rang. Dad answered. "Yes, Meera, both of us are sick. Let me give it to her."

Mom sighed before she spoke to Meera Masi. "I'm so sorry we can't go. This came on so suddenly. When I woke up I was feeling fine. I even made dough because Nina wanted to bring rotis with us."

Then she listened for a few minutes.

"I don't see why not. Yes, that's an excellent idea. They can both go," Mom said.

She hung up the phone. "Nina, Meera Masi says you and Kavita can go with them to the cabin. No sense in all of us being cooped up in the house."

"What if I take the dough and make rotis there? Jay, Kavita, and I can roll them and Meera Masi or Uncle Ryan can cook them."

"Sure," Mom said. She closed her eyes again.

Kavita's face lit up like a string of holiday lights as she dangled a green gift bag in front of my face. *"Yay, yay, yayyayyay, yay, yay, now I can hand out my cards by myself. Yay, yay, yayyayyay, yay, yay, now I can hand out my cards by myself."*

Oh no! My singing sister had returned!

Mom and Dad wouldn't be at the cabin and Kavita and I would be with Team Davenport. I wasn't sure I wanted to go without Mom and Dad because when they are not with us, I feel anxious. Especially in a new place. On top of that, I would need to take care of Kavita. I mean, Meera Masi would feed us and all that, but still, Kavita would be my responsibility. And her singing would be my embarrassment.

"I've already put Kavita's clothes in a suitcase. Are your clothes ready, Nina? They'll be here in fifteen minutes," Mom said.

"Our suitcase is packed," I said.

Dad got up from the couch. "I'll bring it down."

"I'll get the dough," I said.

"Fun is what we're going to have. F for fun, U for us, N for now. Fun for Us, Now!"

Kavita's singing had definitely come back. With force.

My flour-coated finger-crossing from yesterday had clearly not worked.

I placed the dough container in a brown paper bag. Grandpa Joe probably didn't have any rolling pins. I slipped two of ours in the bag. I carried it all to the front room and set it on the window bench. Kavita held her gift bag.

"Put your bag down so you can get your jacket on," I said.

"I can't. If I put it down I might forget it."

"You won't."

She wiggled her right arm into one sleeve of her jacket while holding her bag in her left, then she switched the bag to her right hand and slipped her other arm into the left sleeve. I zipped up her jacket.

After I put my jacket and shoes on, we both sat at the window bench next to our suitcase.

There was no snow on the ground, but the trees were still bare. The grass had turned green, but the sky was gray. I felt just like the way things looked out our window. Without Mom and Dad and with Kavita and her singing, what was I going to do?

"Are they here?" Mom asked.

"You sound better, Mom. Do you want to go?" I asked just in case she had changed her mind.

"I'm not better."

Better or not, she sounded a little annoyed.

"I am sure you'll have fun. Nina, take care of yourself and Kavita."

Now it was my turn to be annoyed at Mom.

Even though she knew I took good care of Kavita, Mom reminded me to do that. She never ever wants me to forget that I am a big sister!

CHAPTER TWELVE

"You want to know what's in this bag?" Kavita asked Jay as soon as we got in Meera Masi's van.

Jay shook his head. It seemed more *no, I don't want to know*, rather than *no, I don't know what's in the bag*.

"It's a secret," Kavita said.

"Then you'd better not tell him," I said.

"It's a secret that's going to come out, so I don't mind sharing it." She leaned across me and grabbed Jay's arm.

I stared out the window even though I was sitting smack between Kavita and Jay.

"Are there any spring songs we can sing?" Kavita asked.

My sister-fixer project had drained away like Lake Ninita. Still, I told her, "There aren't any."

Meera Masi gave me a sharp look through the rearview mirror. "You can sing any song you want, Kavita."

"We could even sing Christmas songs, because it'll be here before we know it," Kavita said.

No one reminded her that it was more than eight months away.

She sang, *"Have a laughy-happy spring, because it's the best time of the year. Say hello to flower friends and every bee you meet."*

Talk about embarrassing!

"Please be quiet," I whispered to her.

Jay joined Kavita in singing.

Talk about weird!

And I had to sit between the embarrassing and weird.

Talk about trapped!

Kavita's singing had spread to Jay and then to me. At the end I had also joined in. That's the real danger of Kavita's singing. It is contagious.

Con-ta-gious means it spreads easily.

After an hour of singing silly, made-up songs we reached the cabin. Jay's grandpa had bought the cabin a year ago and we had not been there yet. They kept calling it a cabin, but once I saw it, I called it a mansion in my mind.

Man-sion means a house where you can invite all the people you know to come in without it feeling crowded.

Uncle Ryan and Jay started to unload some of the luggage. I took our suitcase. As we walked the brick-lined, curvy pathway, Kavita greeted every flower alongside it, and she even bent down and kissed a red tulip.

"Can you guess why I kissed that flower?" she asked me.

I wanted to say, "Because you're crazy." Instead I said, "Because you thought you were kissing two-lips."

"That's so smart," she said. "I didn't know you were that smart."

"I'm smarter than I look."

"Ha! You're smarter than you look. I'll have to remember that." Jay had snuck up behind us, dragging his suitcase.

Ugh!

Grandpa Joe opened the door. "Hello, sweeties," he called out to Kavita and me.

He probably didn't remember our names, so calling us sweeties worked well for him.

"Can I give everyone their cards, please?" Kavita asked. She was still clutching her bag, so I thought maybe it was best if she went ahead and gave out the cards.

"You certainly are a sweet pea, aren't you?" Grandpa Joe said. I bet if he knew about Kavita singing "stomping on the old man Joe" he wouldn't think Kavita was a sweetie *or* a sweet pea.

Kavita nodded in agreement.

The first card was for Grandpa Joe. She had scribbled "Happy Birthday" all over the front. She must have asked Mom or Dad how to spell "birthday" because she didn't ask me.

"How did you know it was my birthday?" he asked.

"I know because I heard my mom and Meera Masi talk about how you are getting up in age and with each birthday it gets harder and harder for you to..." She looked at Meera Masi for help.

Meera Masi's face was as bright red as the flower Kavita had kissed and she didn't offer any help.

"...to...to..." Kavita looked at me.

"Lucky dance," I whispered.

"To Lucky dance," Kavita said.

"What is a lucky dance?"

"Come on, Nina, Jay. Let's show him," Kavita said.

Jay got up. I did not.

"Nina's too shy to do this dance in the house, but she taught us. On a sidewalk," Jay explained.

Grandpa Joe, Meera Masi, and Uncle Ryan looked confused, but they didn't ask questions.

Then Kavita and Jay danced the Lucky dance.

Grandpa Joe laughed and then everyone laughed. Even me.

Kavita handed him one more card.

He read it out loud. "'Happy spring.' How sweet."

If Grandpa Joe said "sweet" one more time, my ears were going to turn into syrup.

"It's from my whole family," Kavita said. She stood by Grandpa Joe and introduced our paper family. "That's my mom resting on the sofa with tissues in her hand. Because she has a cold. My dad is the one with his eyes half-open because he hasn't had his morning tea. That's my sister, and the littlest one is me."

I peeked at the card and saw that Kavita was not the littlest one in the picture. And my stomach was colored yellow. I stayed quiet, hoping Grandpa Joe wouldn't notice my stomach.

Kavita handed cards to Jay, Meera Masi, and Uncle Ryan. I wondered if I was yellow-stomached in their pictures too. I didn't have to wonder long.

"Kavita, this yellow is the perfect shade for turmeric," Jay said.

"That's why I used it for Nina," Kavita said. "Her tummy is still yellow."

Most of the time I love my little sister, even when she is weird. But this was an exception.

Ex-cep-tion means it is different this time.

"Stop it." I wanted to make confetti out of Kavita's card.

It was one thing for Kavita to sing silly songs anywhere and everywhere. But this was beyond silly. Why did Kavita have to draw our family? Why did she have to mention anything about my stomach to Jay's grandpa? Kavita had no right to do that.

"Yellow? Why is your stomach yellow, dear?" Grandpa Joe asked.

Great! Now Grandpa Joe wanted to know why I had turmeric tummy! I could feel my face burning.

I had told Kavita that her art would make our world peaceful and colorful. I was so wrong. All her made-up songs, loud singing, hogging attention was not even close to what Kavita had done today. She was sharing my embarrassing secret with Grandpa Joe. And he wasn't even our grandpa.

"I...I didn't mean..." I was so upset that I couldn't finish my sentence.

Of course, Kavita explained. "Nina's stomach was hurting, so she called Dadi in India."

I glowered at her.

Grandpa Joe looked confused. "Is your daddy in India?"

Kavita shook her head. "No, no. Dadi."

Grandpa Joe repeated, "Yes, your daddy."

Jay calls Meera Masi's mom *Patti*, which means grandma in the Tamil language. I thought that was probably why Grandpa Joe didn't understand.

"*Dadi* means grandma in Hindi," I explained. At

least now the conversation was moving away from my yellow stomach.

Grandpa Joe kind of nodded. I wasn't sure if he really understood what *dadi* meant or had given up on it. I hoped Kavita had too. But she hadn't given up on telling my story.

Kavita went on. "Dadi wasn't home, so Nina talked to Montu. He's our cousin and lives with our dadi and dada and his mom and dad. Montu said to put turmeric on her stomach. So that's what Nina did. Now it is all yellow and will stay that way forever."

"No, it won't," I said. "It's already a little lighter."

"Prove it," Jay whispered.

I glared at him.

"But why is it yellow?" Grandpa Joe asked.

"You remember the spice my mom uses that turns cabbage and cauliflower yellow?" Jay asked. "That's what Nina rubbed on her stomach."

I could feel tears pricking my eyes. Grandpa Joe

looked at me as if I was from another galaxy. "Sweetie, why did you—"

Then his cell phone rang. Very loud. It was Jay's aunt, so they talked for a while. I was relieved. After the call, it was time for lunch.

We made cucumber-tomato-cheese-chutney sandwiches. And ate.

I hoped my yellow stomach was forgotten forever.

✻✻✻

There had been no dark clouds when we arrived at the mansion. But now there were. It began to rain. So much for going out on the lake.

"What should we do now?" Jay asked.

"Let's play board games," Meera Masi said.

Maybe it was because we were at a mansion, or maybe because we were at his grandpa's house, or maybe because his mom told him to, but Jay acted like a mini Grandpa Joe. He was super-polite and extrathoughtful.

"What game do you want to play, Nina?" Jay asked. "You're the guest, so you get to decide."

I shrugged. "I don't care."

"I'm also a guest. Do I get to decide?" Kavita asked.

"Sure. After Nina, you can decide."

"But Nina doesn't care," Kavita said. "How about if we make up songs and sing them?"

"No more. We already did that," I said. I was still upset with Kavita.

"Kavita, how about you pick a board game?" Jay said.

Kavita chose Candy Land. I gave Jay a look. *Do we have to play that?*

Jay smiled. "That's a great game, Kavita. Let's set it up."

Unlike Grandpa Joe, Jay didn't use words like "sweetie," "sweet," or "dear." Still, he was a perfect host.

***

After playing Candy Land, we played cards. Then Meera Masi told stories to Kavita, Jay, and me. They were about five brave brothers called Pandavas who lived in India a long, long time ago. Then we read books Jay had brought from home. Then we watched the rain *plip-plopping* on the lake. Even after doing all that, it was only four o'clock. Even time was *plip-plopping* away too slowly.

"What do you want for dinner?" Meera Masi asked.

I covered my mouth. "Oh, I forgot. I bought roti dough. It's still in the car."

"I put it in the refrigerator," Uncle Ryan said.

"Thank you!" I was happy. "Jay, Kavita, and I can roll them if someone can cook."

"I can do that," Uncle Ryan said.

Good thing I brought two rolling pins because there were none at the cabin, just like I'd thought.

"Do you want to learn to roll?" I asked Uncle Ryan.

"Sure," he said.

I dusted the dough ball with flour and handed it to him. He rolled it so hard that it stuck on the rolling board.

"You have to do it gently, Dad," Jay said. "Like this."

Uncle Ryan tried again. This time it didn't stick but it didn't get much bigger.

"This job is harder than it looks. How about if I start cooking?" he asked.

Jay, Kavita, and I took turns rolling rotis.

Kavita sang to tell Uncle Ryan what to do: "*Slap it on the skillet. Turn over once. Then puff it up. Serve with ghee. Ready, set, chomp.*"

While we made rotis, Meera Masi made green beans with coconut and also lemon rice. The color of lemon rice matched my stomach perfectly, but I didn't mention that to anyone. We ate all the food with creamy homemade yogurt.

*** *

Because of all the rain (there was more in the fore-cast), we weren't going to be able to do any of the things that make being at the lake fun, like going on the boat, swimming, or even looking out at the water. So we cut our trip short and returned home the next morning. I was happy about that.

I mean how long can you act like a perfect host or perfect guest when you are nine? Or even younger? All cooped up in a mansion? Not long. It is the most boring thing ever.

By the time we left, Grandpa Joe had stopped call-ing us sweeties and sweet peas and dear and darling. Because he had enough time to learn our names.

On the way back, Kavita sang, "*Spring, spring, rainy rainy. Tiny tiny, rice-o-grainy.*"

Well, I had failed completely on my sister-fixer project.

The last twenty-four hours were proof of it.

CHAPTER THIRTEEN

When Kavita and I got home, Mom and Dad were feeling and looking better. I wondered if our going away or just being bored had helped them recover.

I didn't have time to figure that out.

It was time to devise a foolproof sister-fixer plan.

I went to my room, opened Sakhi, and again made a list of what I had to fix.

Kavita's weirdness list

* Kavita makes up songs that make no sense.

* She sings these songs.

* She sings them loudly (to attract attention).
* She dances in the street and makes everyone join her.
* She plants rice in a dam (which I also did, but she was the one who thought of it).
* She makes up songs about planting rice. (Sometimes I sing with her.)
* She draws pictures of our family.
* She tells the world about our lives in pictures, including embarrassing details like my yellow stomach.

The list was longer than I thought.

Once I made a list of Kavita's weirdness, I made one about Jay. Just for fun.

Jay's weirdness list
* He acts mean in the morning, friendly in the afternoon. (He did that last Friday.)
* Even though he is a fourth grader, he is friends with a first grader (my sister, Kavita).
* He sings made-up silly songs and dances in the street.
* He picks at his scabs. (I have seen him do that.)
* He is a polite and thoughtful host.
* ~~He has green eyes.~~

I struck off the last one because having green eyes is not being weird. It is just what he has. I wanted to write more about Jay but I couldn't think of anything else.

I read both the lists again and something wiggled in my head.

Megan is also weird.

Megan's weirdness list

* She brings lunch she doesn't like.
* She talks just the right amount at lunch but too much on the phone. (I guess the phone is for calling and when she's on it she wants to talk, talk, talk.)
* Talking on the telephone inspires Megan.

My brain was on a weirdness-finding track.

I thought about how Grandpa Joe is also kind of weird.

Grandpa Joe's weirdness list

* He calls Kavita and me sweetie and sweet pea even though we have perfectly good names.

He usually doesn't remember them.

* He calls his big mansion a cabin. I wonder what he would call a cabin. A hole?

* When Jay is with Grandpa Joe he is super polite. So Grandpa Joe must have some magic. Nice magic.

I looked out the window at Mr. and Mrs. Crump's house. They are weird too. In a good way.

The Crumps' weirdness list

* I thought they were going to be mad at me, but they didn't get mad.

* Mrs. Crump grumbles about Mr. Crump a lot so I was sure she was going to grumble about our dam. I was worried about what she would say when I apologized, but she laughed.

Maybe she only ever grumbles about Mr.
Crump because they live together and are
very retired. I mean, when you are retired
you have nothing else to do, so maybe
grumbling gives her something to do. I'm just
glad their basement stayed dry and I didn't
get in any more trouble.

✽ On top of not grumbling, Mrs. Crump didn't
take back the whole big cherry pie she had
given us. Now that is amazing weirdness.
(I know I'm using amazing here, but I do
like the word and it is free.) A sweet-pie
weirdness.

There were so many people with their very own
weirdness. Like the multiple tracks in my brain.

Wait!

I wrote.

Nina's weirdness list

* Nina likes to discover and build things and ends up flooding a street.

* She forgets her sister at school. (It only happened once, but it did happen.)

* She dances in the street.

* She talks with her hands.

* She listens to her seven-year-old cousin Montu's advice.

* She covers her stomach in turmeric and turns it yellow.

* She sings and plants rice with her sister.

* She tries to fix her sister.

* She makes weirdness lists.

* She even makes her own weirdness list. (How weird is that?)

When I reread all the lists again, mine was the longest and the weirdest and the best.

I wanted to fix my sister but maybe it wasn't possible. People are different. I mean I am different from Kavita and Jay and Megan. If Kavita was just like me, making lists and having too many tracks (and not making up any songs), how would that be?

Even if I made a great plan to change her, I don't think it would work. And if it did, I would be miserable because I would have lost my little sister.

* Kavita, flowing and unstoppable.

* Kavita, poetry in Hindi.

* Kavita, interrupting anyone, anytime, anyplace.

The real Kavita.

I couldn't change Kavita, and it would be difficult to let go of my own weirdness.

I could never ever stop making lists.

I could never ever stop moving my hands when I talked.

I could never ever not have a brain with all those tracks.

My weirdness was me.

I guess everyone has their own weirdness. If all of us were the same, it would be super-boring.

Do you think that? How are you weird? Make a list of all of your weirdness. If you make a list, you will recognize all the things that make you unexpected and fun. And different from other people.

That's what I did. It is good.

I mean, it is good to have a list—and it's good to be weird.

So, double good.

Here is a list of why it is double good to be weird:

* It is no fun to be exactly the same as the next person.
* If you have unique talents (like Kavita and singing), you should use them.
* If you are weird, people will recognize you by your (like list-making Nina, singing Kavita) weirdness.
* It is fun to compare your weirdness with your friends' weirdness.
* All the weirdness makes the world fun and funny and interesting.

I was not going to fix Kavita.

Ever.

Since my *FESTFAS (Five Easy Steps to Fix a Sister)* book was not happening. I made a list of why it was good not to write *FESTFAS*.

In-my-head list of reasons for not writing my book

* There are too many books out there.
* It's more fun to have a weird sister than a blah (Montu would say *bhago*) sister.
* If Kavita is singsong weird, I am list-making weird. I am also sidewalk-dancing weird. But not book-writing weird.

So it is okay to be weird.

It is how we're all supposed to be.

Weird and wonderful in our own ways.

✳✳✳

"Nina, what are you doing?" Kavita asked, standing at my door.

I waved my hand. "Nothing."

She came in and stood by me. "You're making a list! You're always doing that."

"Just like you're always making up songs." I said.

"How about we make a singing list of all we did at the cabin?"

"That sounds like an amazing idea."

She gave me a smile, picked up Lucky, and sang, *"Over the bridge and by the lake, to Jay's cabin we went. Then it rained and it wasn't fair, but we made fresh rotis to share!"*

Then something even more weird happened.

When Mom and Dad asked what we did at the cabin, Kavita and I *both* sang, *"Over the bridge and by the lake, to Jay's cabin we went. Then it rained and it wasn't fair, but we made fresh rotis to share!"*

They clapped. Kavita and I smiled and bowed.

MEET THE AUTHOR!

Kashmira Sheth was born in India and came to the United States when she was seventeen to attend Iowa State University, where she received a BS in microbiology. She is the author of several picture books, chapter books, and middle grade and young adult novels. In her free time, Kashmira enjoys gardening, traveling, and spending time with her family. She also enjoys making lists—but not as much as Nina does! Kashmira lives in Virginia.

www.kashmirasheth.com

Q: Who or what inspired the character of Nina Soni?

A: My daughter Rupa inspired the character of Nina Soni. She is curious, intelligent, helpful, and enjoys doing projects, as does Nina. My other daughter, Neha, inspired Kavita.

Q: Like Nina Soni, you are also Indian-American. Do any of Nina's experiences remind you of your own childhood?

A: There were a few of my childhood experiences that I was able to weave in to Nina's story, like rubbing oil in my hair. Nina and I also share a love of Indian cuisine. In that way there is similarity between my childhood and hers.

There are differences too. Since I grew up in India—in a different time and culture—some of my childhood experiences are not directly relatable to Nina. I used to travel to my elementary school by a horse-drawn buggy and Nina has never ridden in that kind of horse buggy!

I have tried to capture some childhood experiences that are universal, regardless of time and place. For example, Nina wants to be helpful, she worries about Jay and their friendship, and she misses her father when he is away.

Q: Why do you think it's important for readers to be exposed to diverse books written by people who share those identities?

A: Imagine looking in a mirror and always seeing other people's images. That is how it is for many readers who come from minority backgrounds. When these children read books, or watch movies or TV shows, they never see themselves in the story. The message they get is that their journeys are not important or worthy of being told.

When a writer with a particular identity writes a story that includes characters with that identity, the writer knows nuances of the experiences of that group. This richness of knowledge seeps into the story, making it layered and believable for all the readers, and particularly the ones who share that identity. Those readers can see themselves reflected in the story—not as a shallow, stereotypical caricature, but as full, truthful, and meaningful characters.

Q: Many of your stories focus on family. What does family mean to you?

A: Family has always been a cornerstone of my life. I grew up not only with my parents but also with my grandparents, my great grandfather and extended family members. As an adult, I lived not only with my husband and children, but also (at various times in our lives) with extended family members. My mother still lives with me. I love to spend time with my grandchildren now. They keep me connected to my readers, inspire me, and challenge me.

Q: Because your mother tongue is Gujarati, have you faced any challenges writing books in English? What do you find is the biggest difference between Gujarati and English?

A: My mother tongue is Gujarati but Nina's family speaks Hindi at home. Nina's story is written in English. So I get to juggle all three languages.

Each language has its own strength and beauty. It is sometimes difficult for me to find the right word or a phrase in English that I have in my mind in Gujarati or Hindi. At other times there is no cultural equivalent for certain rituals or ceremonies and I end up having to describe them. The same thing happens with food. For example, if someone says I had toast with orange marmalade, most readers would know what the texture and taste of it would be like. If I write I had khakhra (sort of toasted roti) with murabba (raw, sour mango marmalade) I have to explain that. Done too often, it can get tiresome and take a lot out of the story. Done sparingly, it can add depth and richness to the story.

English is rich in verbs whereas Gujarati and Hindi are rich in nouns. It is such a luxury to use different verbs in English to make the action come alive. But describing a physical thing in English becomes harder for me. For example, when I write in English, I keep using the same word for sun or moon, but in Gujarati and Hindi I have several choices.

Q: How have your past jobs inspired your writing?

A: I studied microbiology and worked in that field for many years. It wasn't until I started reading with my two daughters that I thought about writing. My science background seeps into my writing. In *Nina Soni, Former Best Friend*, you can see her mentioning mold and doing a pH experiment with red cabbage juice. I taught dance for several years and Nina takes Indian dance classes similar to the ones I taught.